Christmas With Morris and Boris

Written and Illustrated by BERNARD WISEMAN

SCHOLASTIC INC.
New York Toronto London Auckland Sydney

For Susan, Pete, Mike, and Andy

ISBN 0-590-42434-3

Text and illustrations copyright © 1983 by Bernard Wiseman. All rights reserved.
This edition published by Scholastic Inc., 730 Broadway, New York, NY 10003,
by arrangement with Little, Brown and Company.

12 11 10 9 8   1 2 3/9
           Printed in the U.S.A.   23

Boris the Bear said,
"Christmas is here!
Santa Claus is coming!"

Morris the Moose said,
"Let's ask them to PLAY!"

Boris said, "Christmas is a holiday.
Christmas cannot play.
And Santa Claus will not WANT to play."

"Why?" asked Morris.
"Were you MEAN to him?"

"No!" cried Boris. "Let me tell you why —
Santa Claus is coming late at night.
When he comes he will . . ."

"Oh, I know," said Morris.
"He will go to SLEEP.
It will be too late to play."

"No!" Boris shouted.
"Santa Claus will not go to sleep!
Come with me — I will show you
what Santa Claus will do."

Boris took Morris to a house.
"Look—" said Boris.
"Do you see those STOCKINGS?"

"Yes," said Morris.
"They must be WET.
They are hung up to DRY."

"NO!" Boris roared. "The stockings
are not hung up to dry!
Children hung them up
for Santa Claus. He will come and —"

"I know!" yelled Morris.
"He will come and PUT THEM ON!"

"No! No!" cried Boris.
"Santa Claus will not
WEAR the stockings —"

"Ohhhhh!" cried Morris.
"His mother should MAKE him.
His feet will get COLD!"

Boris shouted,
"Santa Claus has
his OWN stockings!
Santa Claus will come
and fill THESE stockings
with little toys and candy."

Morris said,
"Ask him to bring ME candy
and little toys!"

Boris said, "You must
ask him yourself.
I will show you
where he is."

Morris yelled, "Show me!
And show me how FAST you can RUN!"

"Oh," said Morris.
"Look at that tree.
It has nice FRUIT!"

Boris did not say anything.
He was fat.
He was out of breath.

A boy yelled, "Look! —
A MOOSE and a BEAR!"

Morris said,
"Oh, look at all the CHILDREN."

Boris said,
"They came to tell Santa Claus
what they want for Christmas."

A girl said, "Yes!
Then tonight Santa Claus will
fly in the sky . . ."

Morris asked,
"Does he have WINGS?"

"No!" cried Boris.
"Santa Claus has no WINGS!
He is not a BIRD! Look —"

Morris said, "What is that on his face?
It looks like white FEATHERS."

"No!" Boris shouted.
"Those are WHISKERS!
He is NOT a BIRD!
He flies in a sleigh.
It is like a big SLED.
His REINDEER pull it
in the sky."

Morris said,
"It is not raining.
It is snowing.
You mean, his SNOWDEER!"

"NO!" Boris roared.
"I mean his REIN—"

Just then Santa Claus said,
"Moose, come sit on my lap.
What shall I bring you?"

Morris said, "Little toys
and CANDY!"

Santa Claus asked,
"Don't you want anything else?"

"Yes," said Morris. "MORE CANDY!"

Boris told Morris,
"You asked Santa Claus
for too much candy!"

"No," said Morris. "Look —
I have a LOT of ROOM!"

Santa Claus told Boris,
"Come sit on my lap.
What shall I bring YOU?"

Boris cried, "Medicine!
That moose gave me a headache!"

Santa Claus said, "Don't forget
to hang up stockings."

Morris said,
"We don't have stockings."

A boy said, "I am Billy.
This is my sister, Laura.
Come home with us.
We will give you
stockings to hang up."

Morris said, "I have FOUR legs.
Can I hang up FOUR stockings?"

"No!" Boris shouted.
"People have TWO legs,
but they hang up just ONE stocking!"

Morris said, "I have FOUR legs.
Can't I hang up TWO stockings?"

The children's mother said,
"All right, Moose,
you can hang up TWO stockings."

Boris told Morris,
"You should say THANK YOU!"

"No," said Morris. "I should say
THANK YOU! THANK YOU!"

On the way home
the children's father said,
"Let's sing a Christmas song!"

The parents and children and Boris sang,
"Dashing through the snow,
In a one-horse open sleigh . . ."

Morris sang,
"Dashing through the sky,
In a SNOWDEER open sleigh . . ."

Soon they were home.
Laura said, "That is MISTLETOE.
You are under it.
So, you must get KISSED."

She kissed Morris and Boris.
She said, "Merry Christmas!"

Morris said,
"You mean, Merry KISS-MOOSE!"

Morris and Boris
hung up stockings.
Billy said, "Let's stay up
and see Santa Claus
come down the chimney."

Morris asked, "Why doesn't he
come in the DOOR?
Is he afraid to get KISSED?"

"No!" cried Boris.
"Santa Claus just likes
to come down chimneys."

"Ohhhh!" cried Morris.
"I wish he would
come in the door!
My candy might get
too HOT to EAT!"

Laura said,
"Don't worry. Look —
the fire is going out."

"Yes," said Morris.
"The fire must be tired.
It is going to sleep."

The fire went out.
They waited for Santa Claus.
Morris said,
"I will see him FIRST!"

They did not see Santa Claus.
They got tired and fell asleep.
In the morning the parents woke them.
"Get up! Get up!" they yelled.
"It is time to open your —"

"I know," said Morris. "Our EYES!"

"No!" cried Boris. "They mean
it is time to open our —"

"I know!" yelled Morris.
"Our MOUTHS! I see CANDY!"

"No!" shouted Boris. "They mean
it is time to open our —"

Morris cried,
"I have nothing else to OPEN!"

The parents said,
"Yes, you have! PRESENTS!
It is time to open your PRESENTS!"

Morris and Boris got earmuffs.
Boris said,
"These are nice earmuffs."

Morris said,
"I can't HEAR you with them on.
You mean, HEARmuffs!"

Morris pulled the sled, and
Billy, Laura, and Boris sang,
"Dashing through the snow,
In a one-MOOSE open sleigh . . ."
Morris did not sing —
His mouth was too full.

Everyone opened presents.
Everyone ate candy.
The children's mother said,
"We will be eating
Christmas dinner soon —
don't eat too much candy!
Go out and play!"

Billy yelled, "Let's go out
and ride on my new sled!"

Morris said, "I will hang up
one of my stockings again . . ."